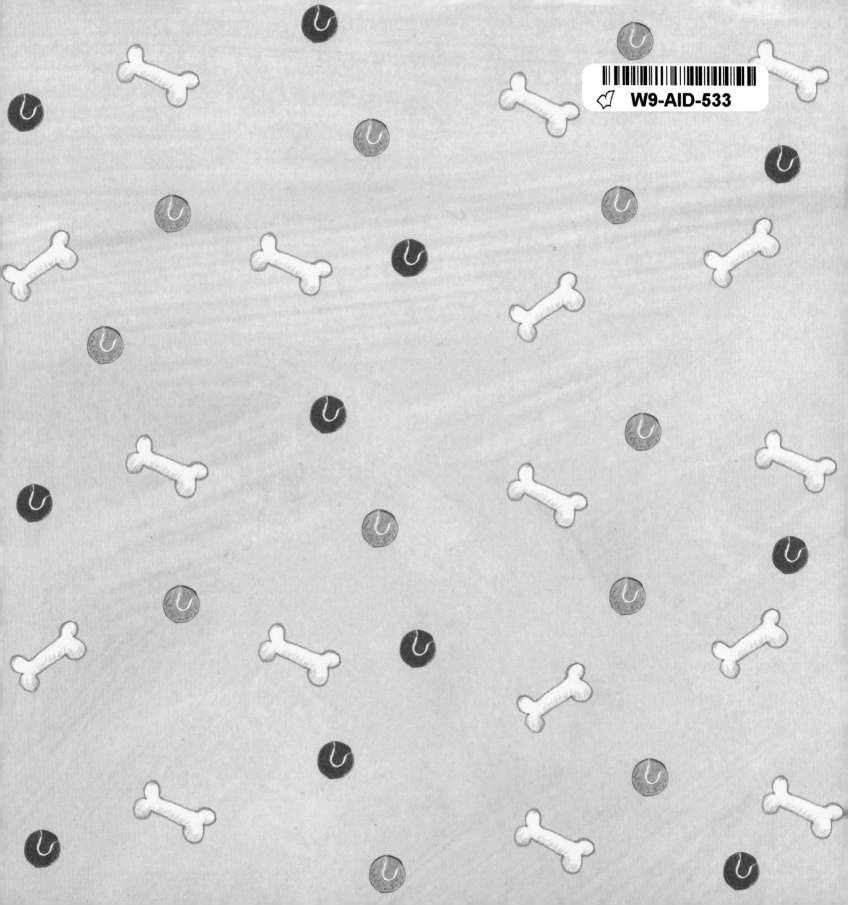

Not Today, Celeste!

A dog's tale about her human's depression

Liza Stevens

with a contribution by Dr Pooky Knightsmith

Jessica Kingsley *Publishers*
London and Philadelphia

First published in 2016
by Jessica Kingsley Publishers
73 Collier Street
London N1 9BE, UK
and
400 Market Street, Suite 400
Philadelphia, PA 19106, USA

www.jkp.com

Library of Congress Cataloging in Publication Data
A CIP catalog record for this book is available from the Library of Congress

British Library Cataloguing in Publication Data
A CIP catalogue record for this book is available from the British Library

ISBN 978 1 78592 008 0
eISBN 978 1 78450 247 8

Printed and bound in China

For my Mum and Dad, with love and gratitude.
L.S.

I used to be the happiest dog in the world.

I had a warm bed, matching food and water
dishes with my name (Celeste) on them,
and a good supply of bones and toys.

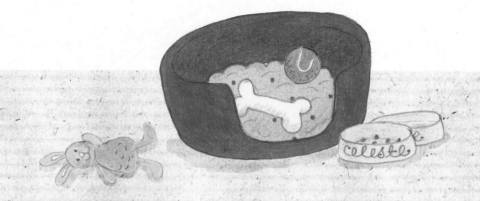

But best of all, I had Rupert.

RUPERT

was:

Kind

Funny

Handsome

Clever

Brave

I had everything a
dog could want.

Rupert and I had each other.

We were happy.

One day I noticed something different about Rupert.
I couldn't quite work out what it was.

Rupert did everything
he always did, after all.

I decided it was just my imagination.

But a few days later, the Something Different was back.

Rupert didn't want to take me for a walk. "Not today, Celeste. I'm too tired."

He wouldn't eat his dinner.

I even had to keep reminding him to give me *my* dinner. "In a minute, Celeste!"

He wouldn't play with me.

"GO AWAY, CELESTE!"

Rupert had never
shouted at me before.

Even when Rupert was trying to pretend everything was alright, I knew the Something Different was still there.

I tried to help Rupert, but nothing I
did seemed to work.

I hated the Something Different. Would it ever go away? Maybe it was my fault.

Would Rupert ever look after me properly again? Did he still love me?

Everything went round and round in my head until it felt like I was going to pop.

I felt:

Lonely

Sad

Angry

Worried

Scared

Then, our neighbours, Lily and Henry, noticed me.

"Hello, Celeste," Lily said.

"You look a bit sad. Is everything alright?"

I started to cry. I tried my best to tell her everything.

Lily came round to see me and Rupert.

She asked me to go to her house to play with
Henry while she spoke to Rupert some more.

It felt nice to play again.

When she came back, Lily explained things to me. "Rupert's poorly, Celeste," she said. "But not in his tummy or his throat or his ear. His feelings are poorly." I didn't know feelings could get poorly!

"The poorly feelings are called depression," Lily went on. "Other people get depression, too. There are people who will be able to help Rupert."

I was relieved I knew what the Something Different was, but I still had lots of questions.

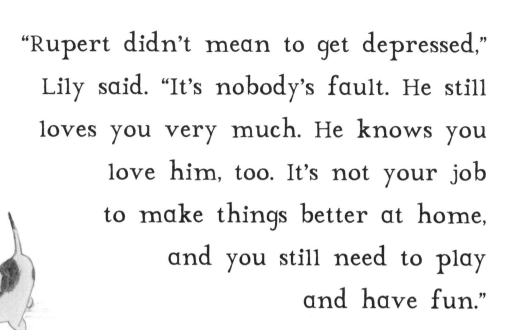

"Rupert didn't mean to get depressed," Lily said. "It's nobody's fault. He still loves you very much. He knows you love him, too. It's not your job to make things better at home, and you still need to play and have fun."

Lily told me I could talk to her any time I wanted.

Rupert did find people
who could help with
his depression.

In time, he started to feel better.

Sometimes I worry that the depression will come back. I know Rupert worries too.

But it won't be Something Different any more.

Rupert and I will know what to do.

Rupert is still

Kind

Funny

Handsome

Clever

and **very,**

very brave.

And I'm still the happiest dog in the world.

A Guide for Parents, Carers and Professionals
DR POOKY KNIGHTSMITH

Rupert and Celeste's story provides a great springboard for talking to children about depression. It offers an opportunity for them to explore and ask questions. It will also make them feel less alone   just as Celeste feels less alone when she learns that other people feel and behave like Rupert sometimes, too.

When talking to children about depression, there are a few things it can be helpful to do.

Help your child find their own meaning for the term "depression"

Discuss the word 'depression' with your child and consider what it means. Use the book as a starting point:

* What signs did Celeste notice that made her worried?

* How did Rupert feel?

* In what ways did he behave differently to normal?

There are lots of feelings associated with depression. Feelings your child will most readily understand include loss, sadness and hopelessness. The difference between depression and having a bad day   which we all have   is that depression lasts a long time, and it stops you doing things. You could talk to your child about what things Rupert's depression stops him doing.

Give your child lots of opportunities to ask questions

You will probably read the book several times. Read it as slowly as you need to. There is no need to rush. Don't be scared of silence and give your child time to consider the story as you read it. If things go quiet, it is possible your child is considering what they've heard and is trying to organise it in their mind, or find the right words to form a question.

Check regularly that they've understood and encourage them to ask questions and explore the story by modelling these behaviours yourself.

Use Rupert and Celeste to explore difficult thoughts, feelings and situations in the third person

It's a lot less difficult to talk about situations in the third person than to talk about them directly relating to ourselves. Rupert and Celeste provide the perfect chance to explore thoughts and feelings through the third person. You can find out how your child is thinking and feeling about certain things by asking, "How do you think Celeste would feel if...?" You can explore how things feel through the eyes of someone with depression by using Rupert similarly, referring to the characters both while reading the story and at other times.

Reinforce the fact that the child is not to blame

Unless told otherwise, many children will assume that a parent is depressed because of something they have said or done wrong. It's important to reinforce that this is not the case. In fact, for many people, there is no specific reason for their depression. It's often easiest to explain it by saying that their brain is a little bit poorly, but it's no one's fault.

Explore how the child can help

Children often feel a lot better once they understand a bit more about depression and they are often very keen to help. Think about ways in which your child might support this can be by saying simple things like, "Cuddles make Daddy feel much better" or "It can make Mummy's head hurt if you're very loud in the house." It's about what works best for your family. Even very young children will often work hard to modify their behaviour in order to support a parent, if only you explore how with them.

10 Key Messages

Key messages that a child living with a parent or sibling with depression can never hear too many times include:

* This happens to other people too you're not alone

* You are loved unconditionally

* It is okay for you to talk about depression and ask questions

* There is nothing for you to be afraid of

* It can get better with treatment like a broken leg

* You have done nothing wrong

* Sometimes depression makes people seem angry it's just because they're poorly

* It is okay for you to have fun and smile

* I am always happy to listen to you

* You should not be afraid to ask for help

All of these messages can be explored using Rupert and Celeste's story.